UP AHEAD

Gordon Carrega

UP AHEAD
© 2014 by Gordon Carrega (carrega@gmx.de)
Photos by Ursula Schorn. Design by Petra Reisdorf
Published by Books on Demand GmbH, Norderstedt
Printed in Germany
ISBN: 9783735757531

CONTENTS

Gordon Carrega lives in Berlin, Germany. He has published three previous collections of prose poems, **Back Gate, A Place to Stay,** and **Life of the Party.** "Days and Means" and "Some Basic Sentiments" previously published by Prose Poem Project. "Clem" previously published by Berkeley Poets Cooperative.

CONFESSION

FOR BAUDELAIRE

Walking through the park, I'm accosted by a well-groomed young man with clipboard and pen poised at the ready who's taking a survey. Would I mind being asked a few questions about my daily habits? I say when it comes to habits I have none because habits are tiresomely bourgeois. I don't rise early and water the plants, drink my coffee on the balcony, walk the dog, do my morning exercises, go south in the winter, smoke a cigar after dinner, call my mother every Sunday, nothing like that. The eager survey taker, seeming disheartened, approaches another random subject, and I proceed with my afternoon stroll through the park, seating myself on the familiar bench in the shady grove, pondering once again the unrecorded history of park benches and their devotees, observing the nearby benches agleam with disuse, supposedly normal people hurrying on by, indifferent to the eternal benches where they could take their place and contemplate the clouds. Today, having put one over on the industrious taker of surveys by refusing to divulge the only habit I do have, though forced to call upon such a paltry word as habit in reference to my daily, sacred presence on the park bench, the very word, habit, awakening a twinge of self-depletion, causing me to wonder if any description would suffice or indeed be at all necessary to depict this recurring moment of bliss, the world turning on its axis of habits and surveys while I behold the clouds and pay tribute to the man who wrote that more than truth, honor, beauty, more even than habits or the opportunity to deceive survey takers, he loved the park bench and the clouds, the clouds that pass, the wonderful clouds.

UP AHEAD

I'm walking, same stretch of road I walk everyday, my destination up ahead. I can see where I'm heading but this morning it's like I'm walking in place, a feeling of effortlessly walking deeper with each step into the same place, not getting anywhere but right where I am, although actually I can tell from my shadow I am moving along. I can see my shadow moving along the ground so I must be on my way, and I stop just to be sure my shadow will stop also and it does. I look behind me, trying to measure my progress but behind me is a long time ago. When my shadow moves I know I'm moving, know I'll arrive for I arrive every morning, can count on arriving. But just up ahead keeps looking the same just up ahead, not getting any nearer, and I'm putting my faith in memory because all the other mornings I've always arrived.

GET GOING

The alarm goes off and, the morning being once again this morning, I'm up, out the bedroom door. Jack, who's staying at my place until he finds a dwelling of his very own, is putting on his overcoat, ready to shove off for his day at the office.

"Leaving already?" I ask.

"Have to get going. See you this evening, and thanks again for giving me shelter."

I drink a cup of coffee and begin the usual ritual of getting ready for the day.

Then Jack returns, enters and sits on the couch, staring at the floor, hands clasped in his lap.

"Forgot something?" I ask.

"I must have. I must have forgotten something. That's surely the reason why I came back."

"Rest awhile and you're sure to remember. I have to rush off."

I am ready to get going and Jack's still contemplating.

"You Ok?" I ask.

"I just need some time to think," Jack says, closing his eyes to help the thought process.

"See you later," I say as I depart.

Strolling along the sidewalk on the way to the bus stop, it doesn't feel right so I turn around and go back.

Jack's exactly where I left him. "You Ok?" I ask.

"I thought you'd left," Jack says, opening his eyes.

"I left and came back," I reply.

"That's what happened to me as well. I left and came back."

"I didn't want to run out and leave you like this. I mean is everything Ok?"

"Don't worry about me."

"I can use another cup of coffee. What about you?" I ask.

"It's getting late," Jack says, standing up, picking up his briefcase, pulling himself together. "I have to get going."

"Won't you stay just a little bit longer? Wouldn't you like to have a cup of coffee with me before you go?"

Jack stops in mid-stride. He turns slowly, looking at me with wide transcendent eyes. "That's beautiful man, really beautiful. 'Won't you stay just a little bit longer? Wouldn't you like to have a cup of coffee with me before you go?' You spoke like... like a divine utterance. Say that again, those same words again."

Jack's beaming at me, waiting.

I'm inclined to shrug off Jack's request but his incandescent expression affects me. I start to repeat myself in the normal way of speaking and then I'm slowing down, hearing my own voice, each word forming with a new significant resonance. "Won't you stay just a little bit longer? Wouldn't you like to have a cup of coffee with me before you go?"

Then I want to speak those words again and again because they gently resonate in me with a fresh delight. Joy is rising in my being, but I manage to control myself. And Jack's taking off his coat like a man luxuriously at peace with the world, setting down his briefcase, the morning settling around us, a radiant, timeless sphere.

PROSPECTS

Memory, plans, looking forward. It's like that echo, that shadow. Keep a diary. One day it will become a book. Such things happen at the right time, preserving the first person, suffering the immediacy. Holding a candle, sifting the evidence, the glossy photos lying around all day awaiting your return as you lurk about, tugging at the edges for a better view. Keep in mind this might be the right time. You might be waiting, you might be missing, you might still be relevant though invisible. You might be the one. And yet the time comes when you're not in the same place at the same time as much as the other guy who's truly contemporary while you're merely on your way to send postcards. One day you'll come back and it will be just like yesterday, even if right now you're traveling unseen in a series of episodes. It is our nature to wonder, to recognize, to call out and be heard. The continual prospects set in our path though we are among strangers. The sky in the old days it all came to nothing.

MORNING COFFEE

Let me do what I must and continue to relish the details that soothe the ever-recurring crisis of being for myself alone, or stepping out beyond the quivering ghostly presences which continue to inform the resolutions I dwell on each day while the ivy just gets greener and greener, more luxurious, more engaging in the sunlight, draping its pleas of sentiment on the frail cashier who's wearing such lovely clothes, and graciously exhibiting the sadness of small change passing from her hand to mine.

SILENT TREATMENT

Several days into our mutual silent treatment we have achieved an elegant civility which in the daily transactions of living together subjugates any expression of anger or displeasure, sharing meals in silence, tersely passing on information as one would be expected to in the interest of good manners, even being social, which allows us to put on a royal glow of normalcy. I see you shining, a porcelain quality, just as I imagine myself to look, while toward each other, when circumstances demand that words be uttered, a matter-of-fact regal hollowness of voice, a majestic stare that includes as well as dismisses, which sums up the challenge, the inclusion and dismissal, the acknowledgement and erasure. We share a commitment to our kingdom, a togetherness that is at the same time denied, the challenge not to throw in the towel, foolishly exiting in fury, not to beg for mercy, not to scream out forgiveness or blame, but to endure, allowing always further refinements of silence to take place, for we have taken on the skilled poise of good players, each of us poised on the brink of a separate oblivion, the argument that must have been the starting point also lost in oblivion. There's something religious in our pretended obliviousness to the other, simultaneous pain and transcendence, every gesture or lack of gesture, every dismal word having a penance all its own, the penance of need and denial, a shared negation of our history, and when the world intrudes and I must be out and about, away from you, my voice becomes wild, strangely gleeful, a solitary hysteria latent in every sentence. A weariness sets in, for I want back into our kingdom of the silent treatment where the only danger is that spark of genuine recognition that can unexpectedly light up the eyes, give to the voice the impulse of the heart, calling us back from the unexplored depths of the vast and carefully monitored silence between us.

HOMECOMING

A taxi gets me from the train station to my mother's house. Positioned on the front porch, frail, hunched over, supported by her cane, her caregiver hovering behind her, my mother's waving, her raised hand, held weakly at shoulder height, gently moving from side to side, caressing the air. My piece of luggage on the ground near my feet, my mother and I wave at each other, suspended in time with this one task to wave tenderly, dreamily. Her slight, innocent smile and wistfully amazed eyes, she seems spellbound by my appearance, my sudden presence right there in the driveway, looking up at her, a radiance to her face, pale and bony that it's become, her skimpy gray hair taking on the look of a halo in the twilight.

Sitting next to her on the sofa, she's having trouble keeping her eyes open, her vague, erratic, elliptical questions about my life, her wispy voice and poor hearing causing me to lean in close. My arm around her shoulder, my mother and I drift into a peaceful haziness where statements lose their factual quality and it doesn't matter if the details hang together. Later, I take my place in the chair by her bed, the caregiver administering the nightly medicine before going into her nearby room, leaving us alone, nothing more to be said. Assuming she's asleep, I get up but my mother opens her eyes, asking can't I keep her company a little while longer? The light by her bed remains on when I do finally manage to get away, mother's nightlight.

Upstairs in the room that I used to call mine, I throw myself on the bed, shutting out the memories lurking about, the photos and mementos on the walls and tables, only to be brought back by the sound of rain pelting against the roof and window panes, strong winds enclosing the house. I go downstairs to check that everything's secure against the weather, and stand by the door to my mother's room, watching her sleep, the word "nightlight" repeating in my thoughts while the storm rages outside.

I figure I'll take my place once more in the chair by her bed, like it's my duty to keep watch until the storm abates. "Don't worry about anything," the caregiver says as she appears in the doorway, her words liberating me. "Go upstairs and get some sleep." I envision how it will be tomorrow when I get into the taxi, my mother standing on the front porch, the two of us waving gently at each other, her futile hand caressing the empty space.

THE BROOCH

I'm walking by a shop that sells costume jewelry. Glancing in, I recognize the girl behind the counter. She used to be a classmate, had dropped out of school, disappeared without a word from one day to the next.

Remembering how we had liked to flirt and joke around, I enter the shop.

Slightly dazzled by all the sparkling objects, I say, "What's a girl like you doing in a nice place like this?" I expect to get a good laugh and be brought up to date but when she glances at me, her indifference knocks the wind out of my sails.

She's perched on a stool behind the glass counter, focusing on the filing of her nails. She's all dolled up, bright red lipstick, bracelets, earrings, necklaces, brooches, and silky clothing. I continue to mutter questions about why she had left school, but her few words, the impatient tossing of her head, her shining hair whirling around her, make everything tedious.

I can't just turn around and walk out, acting hurt and rejected so looking around at the colorful, glittering jewelry, the array of gaudy pendants, bracelets, brooches, I say, "I'm looking for a present." Staring into the mirror right behind her, I take control of my posture, standing tall, my chin raised like a man of the world. "Could you recommend something?"

She sets down her nail file, reaches into the glass case, removing a brooch with a big green stone in a gold-plated filigree setting, placing it on the counter. Staring at the stone, examining the setting like I know what I'm doing, I tell her I'll take it.

She asks if I'd like to have the brooch gift-wrapped? Her voice becoming familiar, echoes of the merry, tinkling quality that had made talking to her the high point of my school day. She actually smiles, looking like she's ready to chat a bit, maybe ask who's the present for, or how are things at school.

But I'm now settled into my self-possessed, arrogant attitude and after she puts the brooch in a box and wraps it up, after she hands it to me, her hand outstretched, her eyes obviously hoping that I'll relent and be friendly once more, I stare at the big rhinestone ring she's wearing. "Nice ring," I say, without even looking at her, taking my gift and making my exit.

The small package stays in my jacket pocket, and the following afternoons after school when I walk by the shop I stride along like a man with a mission, my hand clasped around the gift in my pocket, making sure not to even glance in.

It takes a few days before I begin to change my attitude, to soften up, to realize that she'd been probably putting up a front, for I had surely taken her by surprise, barging in with my silly remark, not giving her time to warm up to me again after all these months.

I get the impulse to go by the shop and give her the brooch, just walk in and hand it to her and see what happens. When I do go by it turns out that she no longer works there, the woman who owns the shop explaining that the young lady had been just helping out from time to time and now she has found a real job somewhere else.

Surrounded by the display of fancy, glittering items, breathing in the woman's perfume, noticing her pearl necklace, her ring that I assume is a sapphire ring, her bird-shaped earrings, noticing that she's wearing a brooch that looks similar to the one I own, I leave the shop and walk along, holding the brooch in my hand, staring at the green stone until my intense staring makes the brooch seem like something magical, and I pin the brooch inside my jacket, to the lining of my jacket.

I keep my jacket halfway zipped so that no one can easily catch sight of my secret talisman, but of course it does happen now and then, the usual mocking hilarity of my friends because I'm wearing a woman's brooch pinned to the inside of my jacket.

On these occasions I become solemn, mysterious, a melancholy romantic forced to endure the foolishness of his fellowman, saying that I'd rather not talk about it but, if you must know, the brooch had been given to me as a keepsake by someone who knew she'd soon no longer be in this world.

JUST GO ON

If I just go on, if I perform my actions with enough quality to fully satisfy those who wait for the results coming in. Taking what I can, outlines of the urge to live admirably, my virile common sense summing it all up right from the start. To endure is more than I know, being always more than the obvious. See me just this way and now just that way. More slowness than memory, more silhouette than ever, and what if you had chosen tomorrow instead of today, would there be a clearer light in here to show me more fully as I ponder my generous wish to share with you all that is precious, speaking from experience, no gushing forth nor preliminaries while the question turns in the air and begins its return.

TEHACHAPI

I get off the bus in front of the Tehachapi Café and as I enter the few customers stare at me while I sit at a table, place my camera on a chair, my overnight bag on the floor.

Stroking my chin, "Could use a shave," I mutter to myself.

While the waitress pours my coffee, I ask her, "Do you know a cheap place to stay in Tehachapi?"

She looks startled, perhaps thinking, "A suspicious character has come to Tehachapi." She says, "The Tehachapi Motel."

My camera captures the ghostly deserted Main Street of Tehachapi, and then the Tehachapi Motel. "Write legibly," I remind myself while registering but I can't fill out the line that says make of car.

"I arrived by bus," I tell the clerk, asking, "What is there for a visitor to do in Tehachapi?"

"Wander in the hills and look at the wildflowers," he answers.

In my room, talking to myself, "A life of rooms and tonight I sleep in Tehachapi, sleep being a place separate from Tehachapi."

I stroll along Main Street, stopping to photograph the surrounding hills. Then in the Tehachapi Saloon, placing my camera on the bar, smiling amiably in reply to the questioning looks, I order a beer, glancing at the waitress in a way that says, "This stranger is mysterious and certainly worth knowing."

More camera work upon exiting, getting the Tehachapi Saloon, ambling down the street, snapping the Tehachapi Café. Crossing the railroad tracks, a good shot of the abandoned railroad car. Sauntering into the hills, holes in the ground under some big boulders, muttering to myself, "Might be snakes in these hills."

Busy with the camera, rock formations, wildflowers, the view of Tehachapi, then a slithering sound behind me and I sense danger in the hills of Tehachapi.

SANDALS

Shaking hands with the sandal maker, the sure, honest hands of a craftsman, then Kay's sitting with him at his drawing board, leaning towards him, her long hair falling over her profile. While he sketches a couple of possible designs for the new sandals I explore the shop, big, intimidating pieces of leather hanging from the beams, tools and artifacts orderly arranged on the workbench, work in progress, handbags, vests, more sandals, a stained-glass skylight directly above the workbench letting in a hallowed light.

The sandal maker, in well-measured tones and with honest eye contact, going over all the details, the elaborate weaving of the leather, the decorative brass buckles, the question being how high on Kay's legs should the leather straps be, certainly not as high as her knees for she doesn't want to look like a woman who's got a leather fetish Kay says with a laugh, and she's stroking her legs to indicate approximately the height she prefers, the sandal maker nodding his approval.

Kay's feet must be measured, the sandal maker accomplishing this task by kneeling in front of her, sitting on his haunches, reverently taking Kay's foot in his sensitive hands, looking up at her, his deep meticulous voice explaining one essential detail after another, Kay sitting back leisurely. Finally Kay deciding to take the designs with her, to sleep on her decision and return on the morrow with her mind made up, and Kay's got the sketches with her in bed, pondering them silently and dreamily, going alone to the shop the next day, paying further calls on her sandal maker for the work in progress must be fitted, adjusted to her lovely feet.

The day arrives to pick up the sandals, Kay trying on the finished product, our sandal maker kneeling in front of her once again, tying the straps that climb up her legs, the leather bindings bold against her bare skin, tightened to her calves. She's prancing around, getting the feel of the new footwear and she'll be wearing the sandals out of the shop, the sandal maker reduced to the task of disposing of her old sandals. Now I'm stooping to admire the sandals, complimenting the sandal maker on the quality of the leather and his craftsmanship, querying him about kinds of leather, his customers, his choice of vocation, getting him talking, Kay standing by, shuffling around in her glorious sandals. We're out of there, the sandal maker waving from the door, Kay sauntering along down the street, hips swaying languorously, skirt swirling around her legs, her laid-back pace in her first-rate hand-made sandals. I look behind us, waving at the sandal maker who's waving in the doorway.

BECAUSE

It's cold in here so the thing to do now is get up and close the window, but I'm waiting because the window looks good swung open in a daring sort of way, and because the fresh air gives me the feeling of participating in a world larger than myself because I'm sure that my neighbours sitting out are pleased to see the window open, whispering among themselves, "Look, his window is actually open." They aren't waiting and wondering what to do next because they're enjoying the sunshine, appropriately dressed for the cool, sunny afternoon, and the open window is part of what is currently happening because sunny weather means open windows, though the fresh air does make it cold in here. Not to mention the breeze rustling the papers lying about, making me sense a ghostly presence in the room with me. Closing the window would mean taking action, remedying the situation immediately, but then all those normal folks contentedly placed in the world outside my window would look up at me and chat among themselves, saying, "Look at that guy! He hardly ever leaves his flat, never joins us in the sunshine, and now he's closing the window which he opened a little while ago. Does he have something against fresh air?" The thing to do now doesn't seem to be wrapping a blanket around myself and waiting for the ghostly presences to reveal themselves because I'm not in the least interested in ghostly presences and because most people don't like to wait and I want to be like most people for whom waiting is not considered a good thing. One hears the expression, "Let's wait. It will be better if we wait," but it's not the waiting that's relished because you want the waiting to be over. You want to have what you're waiting for, assuming you know what that is. Of course I could simply leave the window bravely open, go hide out under the warm covers and then later sneak out of bed and close the window because the window will have been open a decent length of time, the sun will have gone down, night coming on, which always gives me something else to think about because nightfall is, so to speak, an experience well worth mulling over just because I'm always left holding the proverbial bag, exclaiming, "Hey, is that all there is!"

YOU

I go out for breakfast, a place I've never been before, sit at a table in the corner and read the newspaper. I bid the waitress a cheerful good morning and she takes my order. When the waitress comes by again she speaks my name, asking if I'd like some more coffee. I haven't told the waitress my name and I'm ready to ask the waitress how it is that she knows my name but I decide to forget about it and then a man I've never seen before enters the café, addresses me by name and asks to borrow a section of the newspaper. I'm too startled to say anything other than, "Yes, of course." The café is crowded and the customers are all engaged in conversation. Among the words being spoken I hear my name uttered again and again. My name escapes from one person's mouth and then another and another, but no one looks at me and I know that the word which happens to be my name is an accident happening randomly in each mouth. The sound of my name is like a background chant to the general conversation and I tap my hands on the table in time with the rhythm of the chant as I try to keep track of the next mouth to have the accident of my name.

OCCURRENCE

Right now I'm remembering you as you are at this moment, my remembering taking the lead, for even before you turn and look out the window at the gathering twilight, saying "It's later than I thought," I already have you in memory saying exactly those words. Even before I say, "Stay awhile longer," and you answer that you must be going I already have your script in the realm of nostalgia. And then I just know, the way knowing happens between two kindred souls, our eyes calmly ablaze with seeing, our ears graciously tuned to the echo of your words and mine, I know it's the same for you. Your memory's got me as well and I can surrender, our memories merging, running the show. We don't need to endure an added commentary on what's happening for, in the limelight, we've got our roles on the everlasting stage called the past which at this moment doesn't seem to belong to either of us, to no one actually. And the melancholy atmosphere seeping into the room has nothing to do with you and me, for it's time itself relieving us of all complicity. Now by the door, we are like peaceful ghosts, our glances meeting, somehow gently unconcerned about when, or again, or never.

SHADOWED IN THE DIM

Shadowed in the dim unsatisfactory dependence on chance, often I'm early. Sometimes I call at the last minute. People talk endlessly, people stay late. This here's the straight line, the reasonable assurances. Don't spend more than I need to, a standard against which the large, intensely desired, best possible offering, if once performed satisfactorily likely to be called upon again. Everything falling more and more into place, another perfect neck-sized iron ring carefully labeled necessity one-hundred-and-wherever I am in the counting demands of fate. This here's the key, the gracious, precise, well-fondled, and over there, slightly to the left of the piano, that's where I'll put the dead, I mean the deed, when it comes through the door.

TAKING YOU TO THE STATION

Arm in arm we go, down the daily street, for you're going away and I'm taking you to the station. "Have a good trip," the woman next door calls out, throwing open her bedroom window, placing her pillows in the sunshine on the window-sill. "Thank you, I will," you call back in a lilting voice. "She's out of town until next week," I can already hear myself saying, perhaps on the phone. Going in step to the town square, our shadows striding along before us, through the normalcy of the crowd at the weekly market. On the station platform, the other travellers peculiarly still, spaced perfectly apart in their distinct poses, and a sudden absence between us, the familiar intimacy already gone off down the endless tracks, leaving a dullness in its place, a feeling of wanting the parting over with. The train appears victoriously around the bend and you're your lively self again, reaching out for me, saying, "Everything changes once the train comes into view." It's important for you to be in the last car so we're hurrying down the platform, and it feels like an achievement, like we're in a movie, it feels historical, the two of us side by side rushing past one railroad car and then another and another, passing a disembarking passenger, a man alone who looks like he's known too many train platforms with nobody waiting to meet him, folded raincoat over his shoulder, his body leaning to balance the weight of the heavy suitcase he's carrying, going his determined way. You're already boarding, climbing the few steps. I say, "Call me, let me know when you arrive." You remind me of a message I'm to relay to a friend who'll phone and I nod the wise all-knowing nod that says all will be taken care of. People rushing to get on, an announcement for another train, a whistle and the conductor calling out, the door closing, your face behind glass, the reflection of the light such that I can barely make out your image. The train's moving and I'm running alongside, waving, blowing kisses until you're gone in the blur of motion, and, standing in place, I keep on waving, waving like a man sure of just one task.

SOMETHING HAPPENS

Something happens somewhere in time, and I can stare, eyes fixed on any object, maybe the chair until this chair becomes the anything it is, until my presence in the room falls away, the room becoming a room without me, memory taking a step out of itself, forgetting the experience as it happens, wanting to know the message of the wind in the curtains, to hear the clouds talking. Come sky, come on in, just this once give me forever.

COMING IN UNEXPECTEDLY

Your uncanny sense of direction haunts my memory. Nothing where what used to be? Thanks for waiting. We won't meet ever again just like this.

A word almost forgotten: Plight. The barking of a barking dog. Push your luck at the same time each day. I went back again to make sure. Brief candle, no real danger.

If something happens, should be the case. The all-night taxi! You must have noticed how your complete lack of attention neither ends nor begins. Reserved seats at the reservoir against the backdrop of a nameless day.

Here you are back in the world after a long illness. Just think of all there is we can do for one another. Standing right where you are, which way is Texas?

If not today, lonesome for a storm. Make friends, I thought, to make a plan. Time isn't running out, not the way it once was that summer I worked on the ferry boat.

Getting to know all about you, just like I said I would. Dream bullets, these here souvenirs, bullets retrieved from a dream.

What's missing takes my attention on the guided tour. Who you are ends up being never enough and the completeness of never. To think I fear your video camera.

Something shared, a last dance for example. Or a long late night conversation in which a trip is carefully planned. At the last minute isn't a trip. A flag in the distance.

Just yesterday someone I know spoke the word oasis. Right there where right now you're standing.

SOUVENIR

We spend our honeymoon at a hotel on the coast and that first morning she finds among the driftwood a blue-tinted translucent glass ball, light as air and just the right size to be held in her cupped hands. We shelter from the wind in a driftwood shack, passing the luminous object back and forth, investing it with our caressing. The hotelkeeper tells us that our find, a hand blown glass float used on the nets of deep-sea fishermen, signals good luck, and that honeymoon night we pretend it's a crystal ball and take turns staring into our future, making up stories about the happiness that awaits us. Having drunk too much wine, she suddenly has a kind of anxiety attack, the strong roaring of the waves sounding dangerously close. I look out the window, watch the high waves breaking on the dark shore, and report no tidal waves in sight. She lies awake with her hands enclosing the gift from the ocean, holding it clasped to her heart, imagining that the power of the tides have imparted a healing quality to the glass sphere.

The blue glass float, along with the other flotsam called our possessions, bobs along with us for a few years from one apartment to the next, the glass ball usually to be found by her side of the bed among the books, candles, and scattered clothing. Once in a rage, intending to smash this object appearing right then like an accusing eye out of the past, I raise a large volume I have been reading, about to bring it down with all my might, hoping to shatter this relic from happier times. She intervenes, screaming, and I come to my senses. She reaches out for the globe, lies down, holding it clutched to her heart, her way of getting through another hard night. I recline beside her and we recall the stories we had made up with our crystal ball on our honeymoon, all the happiness we had imagined in store for us.

Days later when she finally packs her things to move out, I place the glass float out of sight and in all the anger and chaos she forgets about it. I figure when she notices she has left her sacred object behind she will have a reason to get in touch. I keep the float by my bed and at night, unable to sleep, I cling to our precious find much as she had done, and I keep thinking of all I could have done differently to make a go of it between us.

AGAIN

Changing into loose black garments, the sensation of flowing into darkness. Then closing the drapes, putting out the living room light, my dwelling now without illumination. The lamp on the bedside table not turned on until I make my way to the bedroom which takes place after seating myself in my old armchair. Not settling back to remain at rest, not taking stock of the day, but catching my breath, a let's-be-done-with-it attitude. Getting up, moving along in the well-known shadowiness, peeking through the drapes to spy on the outside world, or pressing my ear against the front door to listen awhile, or leaning against the wall to bide my time, or dashing into the closet, hiding out, or crawling around on all fours, stalking the familiar.

PHOTO PLAY

I've got the photo ready for her when she arrives, the photo I'd taken of the unmade bed after we had made love the last time she dropped by. Looking at the photo, an aura of contemplation surrounds her. "It's all here," she says in a soft, faraway voice, "the sunlight on the unmade bed, the subtle play of shadows among the tangled covers. You can feel the breeze in the curtains. The breeze seems to come from an empty world outside the room, the delicate light creating the sense that the walls encroach and vanish simultaneously, the overall atmosphere one of presence and absence of the lovers who'd had an ecstatic afternoon in this bed. You can feel how they abandoned themselves, the tangled sheets and blankets, the contours of their bodies, their dance of passion remaining although they are gone. I know exactly how you took it. After I'd left you lay in bed, drifting off into a meditative state of bliss. You feel my presence. You feel my absence. You are in an in-between state, a twilight zone of desire. The room is haunted by what was, what is, what will be, and what at some time in the future won't be any longer. You get the camera. You wait for the perfect moment. And then you know, you just know." Then she says, "Something's happening. Can you feel it? Can you feel what's happening?" She takes my hand, her breathing soft, steady, a deep calm settling upon her, eyes intensely alert. Caught in her vision, my senses lifting me outside my usual self, the room possesses a transcendent gleaming quality. "Get the camera, get the camera," she says, "and we'll just wait and watch what's happening to time right now in this room."

CARAVAN

Old friends and newcomers out there in the glimmering. Those of us waiting for news since we last sat together. Or later at home, wondering. Can't wait to read the journals of the crossing.

Do you need night? Shiny surfaces? Red brick covered with ivy? Sun reflected in wine glass? Browsing in bookstores and lingerie boutiques? On our way, merging direction. We wait for the caravan. Knowing consumes knowing.

What is the most recent news of the caravan? We live in that caring. Sickness and death. Darkness and intimate storms. Certainly today I saw a sign. In the sky a large cloud shaped like a camel.

Roses in the garden. The sunshine sits well on your shoulders. Your white silk blouse and musk perfume. Sunglasses again forgotten at the cafe. When you walk down the path to your house, when you enter, as if seen from a distance.

Reflect quietly, the caravan is coming toward you as much as mere intuition. Broken appointments in its wake. After all our plans how could you just get up and go. Name of the game. Sunlight blazes on the church bells. The neighbor sits out and talks to himself.

A question learned with perfect interest. Perseverance daily among sandstorms. Here to receive the dreams of the crossing. Noted premonitions. Sudden whereabouts.

We go about our business. The crowd parts before us. Faces show design. Footsteps and wind. Your summer frock. Empty canteens and sick camels. Some travelers running aimlessly. Love affairs. Some driven to madness by space and sun.

Knowing the sands. Dead reckoning. And those of us who never made the crossing.

DAYS AND MEANS

How to make today disappear into yesterday without having to wait it out? Here's a tried and true method. Distract yourself with the memory of the first time you ever heard the word tomorrow spoken. Feel how your lips open as you reminisce, entranced by tomorrow, tomorrow. Next, make a list of errands. I almost said tasks. Certainly I'm no taskmaster. Nor have I ever been a member of a task force, although I have been known to swagger, in private of course, crossing the room to adjust the volume of the same old jazz. If I were to stop and think about the many occasions I would end up weaving a net around myself, and why not? I should be held in place, shouldn't I?

How easy it is to task the mind. Have you made your list of errands? Errands, the very word cries out for the weather. And once the weather gets into a word you will find eternity in the spaces between the letters. "Be gone," she said. Her last words have accompanied me in my darkness like a cigar poised between my fingers as I gesture wildly in conversation with myself. "Okay," I replied, "I'm out of here. I've got errands to run. A man has to do what he must. See you down the road apiece." This wasn't yesterday but all my tomorrows.

Now back to business. It looks dark from where I'm sitting. Upon getting up I see clearly there's no it. We do, however, have our list of errands. The following ten items will suffice. 1- Please. 2- Do that. 3- Call. 4- Home. 5- Remember. 6- When. 7- Traffic. 8- Ticket. 9- Later. 10- For you. Okay, it's still today. You have an appointment, which is not on your list. You must have overlooked it. To overlook is a good thing. You have an interest in your surroundings. Nor should you look back, being as you are just the shadow of your former self.

At some point the telephone comes in handy. The conversation goes more or less as follows: "Is this you or is it me? Who is it that speaks, who hears my voice? Nonetheless, it's now or never for I'm in touch with myself a lot more than you are. It's enticing to end a sentence with the verb are. About that appointment which we invented, what have you done with it? Did I take it with me or leave it behind? Is it still in the box or still in the dark? I haven't changed a bit since I started out. Thank you." Our list of errands, being errands through which we enter the eternal music of the spheres, and what's a guy to do knowing that he does what he does?

HOLD ON

"Hold on, hold on," I call out, because I've got to say something to my skeleton when it is clearly depicted up there in the wide blue sky, all the other negligible clouds forlornly drifting by. But what's to be held on to when nothing is needed? Skull, spine, limbs magnifying along in contrary cosmic directions, arms opening to embrace infinity, and in smoky anatomical detail the hands reaching down, welcoming me to the universe.

LEANING

I step in front of the strong affable-looking fellow striding toward me on the crowded sidewalk and explain that I'm ready to collapse, would he allow me the opportunity of leaning on him?

Taking a quick look at his watch, muttering about having time before his luncheon date, "Please, go right ahead. I have a few minutes to be leaned on." He takes a strong, upright stance and I begin my leaning.

"Leaning on you is preferable to falling at your feet, causing you to stop and call for help, most likely missing your next engagement, or maybe stepping over my fallen body, continuing along, having me on your conscience all day."

"Lean a bit more if you need to."

"I'm leaning quite enough, thank you."

All around us the usual pedestrians, mothers and baby carriages, shoppers, business people on their lunch hour, a little boy asking his mother, "Mamma, what are those men doing?"

"Would it be better if I assisted you in moving to the bench at the bus stop where you can sit awhile?"

"I don't want to sit down. I just need to lean on you. Next you will be suggesting that I lean against a lamppost, or a tree, or the side of a building."

"No offence intended, for this is the most useful I'm likely to feel all day and it's satisfying to be leaned on right here in broad daylight."

"I'm getting a bit stiff. Could you assist me in changing my leaning position?" His arm around my shoulders, I shuffle around, finding a more convenient posture for my leaning.

"I've taken up enough of your time. Here comes another candidate. I'll flag him down and ask him to take over."

"No hurry. I'm enjoying being leaned on."

"I don't want you to be late for your appointment. Excuse me, my good fellow," I call out to the approaching stranger, "do you have a moment? I need to lean on someone and this guy has done his good deed for the day. Would you mind taking over? The alternative would be my dropping to the pavement."

"I won't let that happen," says the man I am currently leaning on, who is about to be made redundant.

"Glad to help. I'm just strolling about so I could use some purposeful activity," replies the newcomer, moving closer. "Transfer your weight to me. That's it. You're doing fine. Lean on me all you want."

The first Samaritan, seeming abandoned, "Hate to simply run off."

After I assure him he has fulfilled my requirements, he goes his way, leaving me with his replacement, and he turns to wave one last time before being swallowed up by the afternoon crowd.

SOME BASIC SENTIMENTS

The situation depends on the circumstances. The boundary where one situation ends and the other begins. As resolute as perfume, what do you look at besides the clock? Seeing you as you never see yourself promotes nostalgia.

The again that contains the never again. The eternal recurrence of never as event. Futile, yet we went on even further into the futility until we got good and used to it.

Sleep without anybody asleep, pure sleep. Serve my needs, my served needs.

Equally satisfied in our voluptuous yearning for extinction, she explained her cure for jet lag.

Narrative is helpful when giving directions. We were equally careless. The use of black in black and white photos. More or less?

The particular sounds made by someone as this someone prepares to go to bed. Who danced with him before he died? Reasons made of ivory, piano keys, for example.

Come in and make yourself comfortable. I'll come in but I don't know about making myself like you say I should. Come in and make yourself inevitable.

Sleight of hand, the shadows' sleight of hand. First the verdict then the sentence. We'll return later for the cobwebs.

The situation perfectly understood, I went to the party dressed as a door. We compared mistakes, a collection of broken arrows. It was midnight or something similar.

The cure for envy is admiration.

An empty room except for a wooden chair and a life-sized map of the world pinned to the wall. The ballet dancer was the sole survivor of the avalanche.

History of the art of forgetting, earliest records, rituals. Paralysis in a dream, dream paralysis. Serious enough to take notes. The illustrated book of chains and its many uses.

I thought it was just me but it's you also. In fact everyone I've spoken to. That there on the candle it's a flame while this here in my pocket it's a key. I held the key close to the flame.

REPLAY

Our café get-togethers lining up like stepping-stones in the long narrative through the years, meeting for a few glasses of wine and conversation having become enough of an occasion. Tonight he's drifting off more than usual into the troubled silence incurred by his own dilemmas, and if I blink my eyes, imitating the shutters of a camera, I'll see specific images superimposed from memory's darkroom on the screen of tonight, the radiant portrayals of other nights just like this one.

The night winding down, maybe more to be said, a sudden gush that sometimes transpires. His phone call earlier sounded urgent, "Can we meet tonight?" And together we form a balustrade to keep each other from falling too far into what cannot be easily uttered. The waitress saunters about in her high heels, overseeing matters, vigilant eyes and quick responses. The dying fall of the soft jazz and a kind breeze wafting through the café like an expression of gratitude to the other guests for their walk-on roles in our ongoing tale.

Finally we will leave together and before going our separate ways find something to joke about, perhaps his saying he promises to brush up on his conversational repertoire, and I'll ask what kind of friend would I be if I couldn't read his mind? And his mock surprise, "You read hieroglyphics?" Laughing, we'll go our separate ways, calling out we'll be seeing each other soon, our voices echoing in the night.

Now the waitress gives me a quick thumbs-up as I signal her to bring more wine, my old friend's eyes livening up, and I'm in the limelight, saying, "Let's stay awhile longer?" His answer, a vivid smile, a tender shrug.

OF DEATH AND ENVY

When I get the tidings that dynamic, successful, super Joe Smith has kicked the bucket my first thought is goodbye Joe as far as envy is concerned, the irrelevance of envying someone dead and gone wafting through my being, an easeful breath from the hereafter. But the courier, a past acquaintance encountered by chance on my afternoon stroll, doesn't know the details, for he got the dispatch from someone else, neither of us having seen Joe in years.

The familiar envy returning, the weighed down misery, ready to doubt the fact of Joe's demise, I'm peering for traces of uncertainty in the bringer of this info, pinning him down. Yes he's sure, Joe Smith is no more. The place in my brain where envying Joe had been a regular disgruntled prospect over the years becomes radiant and spacious.

I'm saying we're talking about the same Joe Smith who etc. etc., listing his achievements, same old Joe who could usually be counted on for a celebration, his having had so many reasons to rejoice. This ambassador who has appeared to teach me that the Great Beyond gulps down all envy, he's taking on the angelic demeanor of a being appearing out of thin air, saying yes, yes, same old Joe.

Sweetness of the air embracing me, the distressing memories themselves becoming wistful. Back then in this earthly realm, parties in Joe's swanky apartment with me imbibing too much of his top-notch liquor, straining to be the life of the party, skulking out the door just when Joe, the dominant Mr. Charming, was beginning to magnanimously let loose. Then brooding on the walk home, the years extending into one long stroll, paved with envy, away from the actual presence of Joe Smith.

Now, choking back sorrow for both my resentment and the loss of dear old pal Joe, once more for the very last time, are you sure, dear illumined messenger, that we're talking about the very same Joe Smith?

DARKNESS OUTSIDE

Dark night outside, dim light in here. I'm standing a few steps away from the glass door to the balcony watching the reflection of myself suspended within the outer darkness, the spectral figure very much at home in the duplication of my familiar dwelling. The sparsely lit room reflected with the same chaos of books, papers, clothing, as if it would be easy enough for me to make a shift, melting eerily through the glass, stepping into the other dimension so commonplace it appears. Not a mirrored image, for a mirror gives a certain I'm-right-here sensation while this image provides an obscure I'm-out-there-somewhere-in-the-dark-unknown quality. Moving too close I see the trees, the houses, the street, but backing away further into actual space I have once again my alter ego imprinted on the alluring darkness in that ethereal room where this cordial host comes to greet me, comes only just so far because he can't come in, waiting for me always out there.

PYRE

The moonlight making itself at home through the windows of my beach bungalow. White curtains billowing ghostly in the balmy ocean breeze. The shadowiness taking on a blissful glow seeping into my bones. Lulled by the waves gently lapping on the shore.

Voices rising up from the beach. Transported on the melody of the tide. Becoming more distinct as my hearing embraces them. Familiar voices and laughter echoing down the byways of memory. For stories are being told, reminiscences in which my name is repeated.

The eternally soothing hush of the surf making the narrative clear. Faces of old friends appearing in my vision. My own words chiming in with further details. Whispering along to myself. Soft laughter rising in my throat.

Getting closer in the moonlit night. My whole being aflame with the mystery of what's in store. Keeping my distance behind the dunes. Not wanting just yet to break the rapture enveloping me by indulging in handshakes, embraces, and the usual banalities about the passing years. The ocean, a shimmering blue illumination all the way to the horizon. The star-studded heavens gloriously bearing witness to that old gang of mine.

Accompanying sounds of driftwood being placed one piece on top of the other. Each of my long-lost companions adding a log before contributing to the ongoing remembrances. Faces glowing in the moonbeams which have become a spotlight accompanying my eyes. More comrades coming down the beach dragging pieces of wood to be added to the preparation of the bonfire that will no doubt soon be set ablaze.

My sense of duty does require me to go among them. But now they are turning their backs. Departing all together down the radiant beach. Vanishing in the illumined night. Leaving me alone with my memories. The pyre remaining.

GETTING IT RIGHT

She's getting dressed, slipping on her red high heels. Trying on one blouse after another. That sensual indifference of not caring she's being watched. Taking a leisurely pleasure in herself. Primping before the mirror, leaning toward her reflection to get the lipstick just right. Wraparound skirt, billowing folds of sheer material tossed around her hips, flaring about her legs. Another look in the mirror, her fingers undoing the top buttons of her blouse. An indifferent Hmmm in response to my interest in her new perfume.

After the party, back at her place, my behavior offends her, for I have drunk too much, and she's imperiously displeased, will not tolerate my aggression, my being deaf to her wishes.

It's not her words so much as her conviction, her precision, the piercing, petrifying stare. Her hands akimbo, head raised and shoulders back, shifting her hips to support the thrust of her remarks. Glaring eyes and contemptuous tone as she orders me out the door.

In the next weeks, during which she refuses to see me, I can't help replaying this closing scene, compelled to get all the details just right. The image of her branded into my vision, and when she and I finally do get together again of course she's not at all that terrible woman who had appeared to pass unrelenting judgment. I can only feel a puzzling disappointment, a haunting nostalgia.

ENGLISH

Traveling alone in the Himalayas, cold and hungry, lost in the high mountains, desperate and shivering in the piercing winds. The way back and the way forward shrouded in clouds. At night curled in my sleeping bag, huddling in one small cave or another. Doing whatever I can not to awaken panic. Shutting off all inner dialogue until the only language I know is the screaming loneliness of the mountain peaks in which I struggle along like an android, whereabouts unknown, precipices and jagged heights beneath the indifferent heavens.

Finally descending, staggering into a clearing, a cluster of huts, the word help stuck in my throat. I'm surrounded by villagers, all of them wrapped in colorful hand-woven clothing, happy people speaking a soft impossibly musical language. An old man stepping forward, his wrinkled, leathery features full of fatherly kindness, he speaks one word, "English". The word thrown first at me and then to the others who repeat in an eerie rhythm a word sounding vaguely like, "English, English," and I collapse in his arms.

Covered with animal skins, awaking in a hut. Food and drink, the mountain tribe around me, their incessant whispering like a breeze passing among them. Their wide, dark eyes brimming with kindness. Their smiles assuring me that they are having a good time. The one word I can barely grasp, "English, English," passing from mouth to mouth like a delicacy.

The paternal figure, like a man playing charades, graceful movements, repeating the one word, "English", gesturing to impart that someone will come from far away to speak to me in English, pointing at me, pointing at his own mouth, saying "English, English," pointing to the door, pointing in the distance, acting out the arrival, performing the message that I must wait and be patient, one day the arrival will surely occur.

I'm afraid to hear my own voice, to break the spell of suspended hope, bring all the terror I've been holding at bay tumbling down upon me, entering a state of delirium.

Waking up alone in the hut, stepping outside, the whole village asleep, the alien sky, the gloomy summits awakening the dread of being lost forever. Panic beginning to engulf me.

The next day, waiting. The protective patriarch coming again to offer assurance, gesturing to affirm that someone who speaks English will indeed be arriving. Days and nights blending feverishly one with the other. The constant uncanny chatter all around me adding to my frenzied shivering.

Finally the kind elder leading me out, supporting me. A woman approaching slowly, gracefully in long flowing clothing. The tribe parting, making room for her, then closing behind her, following like a flock.

Radiant smile, glowing eyes, she stands before me. All is silence, the woman focusing on me like a goddess come to save me. Tears of gratitude welling up inside me. We'll sit and talk together. I will tell her of my terror, my dreams, my wishes. I am bowing, ready to collapse at her feet.

She speaks, "How are you?" Her voice unbearably loud, louder than seems possible for such a slight figure. A perfectly cultured, queenly British accent, her words resonating. The villagers repeating in their own cadence, "How are you? How are you?"

Compelled to answer, to take refuge in custom, to participate in this ritual greeting, I manage to utter in a quaking unknown voice, "Fine thank you." Once again the villagers' resounding attempt to imitate my words.

The voices fade, a deep stillness sets in. "Very fine?" she asks again in an even more imposing intonation, and then turning to the crowd, orchestrating the repetition, the bizarre chorus of "Very fine" rising to the mountains.

"I'm lonely," I shout, opening my arms to plead for whatever relief this goddess can offer, falling to my knees, "lonely, lonely, lonely." My pitiful cry going on and on, going back through time and space to reach that anguished version of myself, astray and hopeless in a merciless terrain.

The woman, raising her arms to silence the "Lonely, lonely, lonely," seemingly mocking repetition of the clan, their gleeful laughter at tasting words that have no meaning for them.

She poses imperiously before me, "Very lonely?" she asks in a bellowing, majestic tone, and the clan joining in, their ominously incomprehensible version traveling on through the relentless landscape.

WHAT'S TO BECOME OF YOU

I've already become the answer to what's to become of me and I miss the blazing eyes that once threatened with that very question to scorch me wriggling on the wall, the swagger I'd have to take on to keep myself upright. Now with the old boy, my dear father, he's dazed, barely able to keep a spark in his eyes while he tries to focus on his only son.

In some chamber of his memory he grasps that I haven't lived up to what he had in mind for me, back when his mind knew he hadn't lived up to what he had once had in mind for himself, back when he knew how to browbeat me with, "Boy, what's to become of you?" Now I don't have to strut my stuff but simply seek refuge in the armchair across from his rocking-chair where he drifts into his particular brand of nowhere, certainly not anywhere I am because though I can drift off as well I'm still here with mind enough to know he's here in the flesh.

I take the bottle of what used to be his favorite whisky out of my shoulder bag, pouring us each a shot, his eyes embodying a trace of glimmer, "Want a drink?" I ask.

Detecting the glass held out to him, "A what?" An expression of distress, for he's laboring to drag an admonition or two out of his dark cave, managing with, "You're still drinking?"

I tap my fingers on the bottle, "Father and son hitting the bottle together, both of us too old to know any better. Remember how you used to toast your gathering of friends, 'First for the day and the good Lord knows it just like he knows I'm a born liar'? Just one for the road, always one more for the road, that long lonesome road, right Dad?"

His lips are moving, singing along with his old sayings, his face glowing with benevolence, for he's seeing before him the person he used to be while we drink to the years that have taught us to be so similar.

LATER

This rusty iron-gate mounted on a frame of old weathered oak! Take the whole contraption home with you and set it up in your living room. You can open the gate and walk through anytime you choose, the creaking hinges, soothing to your ears as you enter the zone of later.

How about this rose of later? Once in a while just stick your finger on one of its many thorns, let a few drops of blood fall on the petals, and this rose of later will be yours forever. If you should ever forget to feed this rose of later you will dream only of roses and they will all be weeping for you the blood of later.

For the silence of later, perhaps this heavy brass bell? In all aspects a completely normal bell. Sure it's heavy but the weight helps you to swing your arm, swing the bell back and forth. Does the bell ring out the striking as you hold it and swing your arm? Of course it doesn't. That is one of the many silences of later. This silence has a particularly magical effect because you work hard, swinging the bell of later and no sound, no sound.

Now we have this calendar of later. You can of course record all your appointments and the day you expect to arrive simply falls off the calendar, falls into The Nowhere, not even into Eternity, for Eternity, as you must know from your reading of the philosophers, eternally repeats itself but in The Nowhere this day is lost forever.

A bicycle of later? You want to get to somewhere else? The physical, joyous exertion of pedaling furiously to arrive on time, and the somewhere else will always be a vast snowy field, trackless in all directions, not a trace of arrival. And you will always be right on time.

In the cave of later you will find the shadow of your former self. In his hands he holds all the goodbyes you have ever spoken, all the endings you have ever endured. Look, there's a fire! The shadow is hard at work, burning all the goodbyes, all the endings, the smoke turning into the smoky wing of later hovering above you.

BROTHER'S FUNERAL

I'm shopping for a new dark suit of the finest material and appropriate cut to wear to my brother's funeral, investing also in white shirt, tie, and shoes, all of the highest quality because my brother dressed in nothing but the best. I keep asking myself why I hadn't thought of this procedure before my brother's death, hadn't submitted to his penchant for good fashion and purchased an outfit that he would have approved of, gotten all dressed up, dropping by to visit, thereby keeping the familial bonds intact. For my brother and I had never indulged in a bitter falling-out nor any enduring fraternal conflicts, the only problem being his tendency to blurt out remarks like "It's the way you dress, that's why you've gotten nowhere in life," or "Where did you pick up those garments you have on, in the Salvation Army bin?", or "Must you embarrass me by appearing at my place of business looking like hobo?"

While I stand in front of the mirror, the tailor fussing about to be sure of the specific adjustments, the recollection of my brother's ranting seems from a bygone era, having nothing to do with this shining image of myself reflected back at me. On the day of the burial, taking all the time in the world to get elegantly decked out like a man should be in honor of his brother being laid to rest, looking in the mirror, chuckling to myself, savoring the refined coolness of the stylish material against my skin, fixing my tie, getting my hair just right.

Arriving finally at my destination, I'm aghast to discover how late I am, for the casket, accompanied by the thunderous tolling of the bells and the fearful grief-stricken blaring of the organ, is already being carried out, my brother's family and big-shot associates forming the band of stately genuine mourners following along behind the pall-bearers, proceeding with proper solemnity through the cemetery, down the tree-lined path to the gravesite.

The eternally doleful music, the knowledge of exactly for whom the bell tolls making me weak in the knees, the vanity that has caused my late arrival stripped away, I can only take refuge behind the trunk of a shady tree by the door to the chapel, the procession getting ever farther away, going now round a bend, lost among the tombstones, and I refuse, simply refuse to be the elegantly dressed brother of the dearly departed running after them, tearfully crying out, "Wait for me, wait for me."

FATHER RETIRES

I arrive at my father's house and find him sitting alone on the veranda, staring at the sea. "My son! Have you come to add to my sorrows?"

"Now that you are retired I thought you might have some extra time," I reply.

"Time," he says bitterly. "Yes there's time. I've never learned to swim."

"You were the captain of a great ship. You sailed the world," I say, hoping to cheer him up.

"That means nothing now. The sea mocks me because I've never learned to swim."

"I've tried to swim but something stands in my way," I say to my father, adding enthusiastically, "It's not too late. I can teach you."

"Don't be ridiculous," my father says. "You've just told me that you also can't swim."

"I told you that something stands in my way. I need your permission."

We go down to the sea, walk out on a long pier. My father rests his hands on my shoulder. "Swim," he commands.

I jump into the water. My father stands at the end of the long pier watching me swim. He raises his arms high above his head in a victorious salute. I swim way out in the sea. When I look toward the pier my father is barely visible so I turn back. I'm far from shore and I'm treading water to rest a little while. I'd like to witness once again a victorious salute from my father but I see a launch at the pier, my father climbing aboard the launch. The launch begins its journey out to sea. As it goes past me I see my father among a group of men, all wearing their captain uniforms, and they are drinking a toast to my father.

The launch goes to a ship anchored a short distance away. My father and the other captains all climb aboard. I swim to the ship, tread water, call out to my father. Sailors stand at the railing on deck. They laugh and throw scraps of food at me while I plead with them to call my father.

Finally he appears. "What seems to be the trouble?" my father asks.

"Father, why didn't you wait for me? I can teach you to swim."

"Excuse me gentlemen," my father says to the other captains gathered around him, "but I must have a few words with this young man. Let us forget about swimming," my father says to me. "Swim away. Go to my house if you must. But this is no time to talk about our swimming." It is night when I enter my father's house. Water drips from my body as I sit in his chair on the veranda. Staring out at the dark sea, I search for the lights of the ship I know is anchored out there.

THE LOOK

The first time I meet the ravishing young woman who has moved into the apartment next door she's in the company of her handsome husband who is also in residence. I give them the look that says you can count on me to be easygoing and to have neighbourly understanding for the needs of youth and beauty. After giving her the quick once over, I give her the telling look of how easily she'd be able to bring out the lecher in me. Then I quickly add the suave look which says I'm a man of experience and she can count on me not to have any ill-considered, indecent notions.

I give the husband the man-to-man look, sure must be great having such a knockout beauty for a wife but I am old enough to know that, sadly, there are always problems. And I give them the extra look of what a blessing it is to be in the presence of such an enchanting couple who glow like celebrities. These looks become more or less the standard procedure whenever we encounter each other in the process of coming and going and we share the look that says although we're a mutual admiration society we know it's always best for neighbours not to get too chummy so let's be sensible and keep our distance.

One Saturday morning I see him moving out. I keep out of sight and keep all my looks to myself. The next time I see her she seems cheerful enough and I give her a placid, considerate look, a cross between inner wisdom and the look of a neighbour who doesn't need to know all the details but who by his simple presence is a harbour of stability in changing times. I offer her just a wee bit of the reckless look which says now that you're alone in the evenings if you ever get lonely I could be a shoulder to cry on, adding a rational look that says let's not get carried away with our mutual availability and do anything foolish.

One evening I meet the husband while he's paying a visit to the home where he once had known joy with his lovely wife. They seem on friendly terms and I give him the life is suffering look, tempered with the look that says a young fellow like you should simply go ahead and have a hell of a good time. Then I give him the commiserating look of you'll get over it.

The new boyfriend arrives one evening at the same time I'm getting home and he also has that certain glow of glamour. With sprightly self-confidence, he climbs the stairs ahead of me, standing at her door waiting to be admitted. I quickly disappear behind my closed door, but not before I have given him a cordial but stern somewhat fatherly look, you'd better treat her right, or else.

In the morning, the three of us leaving our apartments at the same time, I give her the knowing look of the worldly older man who simply hopes she isn't making a mistake, and quickly add the look that says life's not worth living without a good measure of youthful folly in the name of passion. I give him the look that gives the same message I had given him the night before, adding a look with a slight touch of melancholy which says I too can remember such tender mornings after the passionate night before.

SATYR

Visiting my father in the hospital after his stroke I find a man transformed for he looks like the proverbial bright-eyed lecherous old goat, and his nurse perched on the edge of the bed must find him entertaining because they're laughing together as I enter, sitting myself in the visitor's chair.

Father, casting a swift look in my direction, greets me in a throaty, peculiarly lilting and enthusiastic voice, "My son, the man without woman." His enthusiasm's directed at the nurse, and the nurse, seeming all ablaze, gives me a distracted smile.

The bed raised hospital-style, her arm stretched over his slight sheet-covered form, bracing herself, her legs crossed, the hem of the white uniform having worked its way up, my father's hand resting on her thigh. "This is woman, my son. I've had plenty of these beauties in my time."

The nurse in an intimately consoling voice saying she will leave us alone and return shortly but father prevents her departure. "I feel desire surging through my veins. This old man can't wait too long. This boy wants to learn my secret. All his women leave him, a sad tale but true. Either you have it or you don't."

Tufts of hair sprouts from his almost bald skull, his big ears out of proportion to his gauntness, his should be a sadly comic face but there's an aura around him as if he has tapped into a freely flowing cosmic erotic current. "Couldn't even find a beauty to bring with you to entertain your dear old father, could you?"

The only words I can muster, "How are you feeling, father?"

"I know the truth, all his women leave him."

The nurse looking at me, her eyes seem to be saying, "What harm is it to play along with him?"

"Speak to this woman. Melanie. Melanie. Melanie. Melanie," his voice, soft, rhythmic, muted passion, casts a spell of pure desire, "Melanie, Melanie, Melanie."

"I'm right here," Melanie whispers ever so coyly, glancing at me, moistening her lips, giving me a wink to let me know this is simply a part of her bedside manner, her way of being a good sport.

"Speak to her son. Let me hear you try to seduce her. We'll give you advice. Melanie, Melanie, Melanie."

The nurse is certainly spellbound. Our eyes meeting, I feel a vibration passing between us, a thrill, a daring. Father's voice wavering, his eyes hazy, he passes out.

The vibrant silence in the space between Melanie and me, she straightens up, removes father's hand from where it rests on her leg. Her own hands fluttering, one hand as if to fix her hair, the fingers of her other hand lightly passing over the buttons of her uniform, she prepares her best professional face.

My father's libidinous voice is still in the air around us. "Melanie, Melanie, Melanie." It's me! I am speaking. My father's voice but it's me, entranced, "Melanie, Melanie, Melanie." The nurse tosses a mystified look as she goes out the door.

THE AXE

The rain stops and I get out of bed gently so as not to disturb Cheryl, dress warmly and go outside, uncover the woodpile, chop wood, gather as much as I can carry, bring in the firewood and dump it by the fireplace.

By the time Cheryl comes out of the bedroom in her red woolen nightie and sits on the couch the fire's blazing and a fresh pot of coffee has already been brewed. "Voilà! That's entertainment!" I say, gesturing grandly at the raging fire.

Cheryl's deep in thought so I say, "I love your nightie. I knew we were in this for the long haul that first night when you said, 'I hope you don't mind but I always sleep in a nightie.' It was the way you said nightie. The first night together and you used the word nightie. Do you get my drift?"

"I had a terrible dream," Cheryl says, "a dream about an axe."

"What kind of axe?" I ask.

"An axe, a normal axe, just like the axe you use to chop wood."

"An axe is an axe is an axe," I say.

"But in the dream I was possessed by a demon and the demon was urging me to pick up the axe which was in the corner of the room."

"Which room?" I ask.

"I don't know which room. Maybe this very room, but the axe, the axe is very clear as if illuminated by some terrible light. A demon possessed me and I felt like I would run amok because the demon was saying to me, 'Kill, kill, kill…'"

"Didn't you question the demon? Didn't you … axe … why you should do such a terrible thing?"

"Don't make jokes. I had a nightmare and I haven't recovered yet, this feeling of being possessed by violent urges!"

"Another case of axe possession in dreams," I say. "How about some coffee, and how about…" I get up quickly and take a bottle of brandy out of my desk drawer. "How about some dream medicine?"

"I'm still scared," she says.

"That's what they're for, these night horses, to scare you."

"I was going to pick up the axe. I was on the verge of running amok."

"You're safe now. I just rode up on my stallion. I'm your hero."

"Give me some coffee."

I pour her coffee and say, "Have you noticed my fire?"

"It's a good fire," she says.

"How wonderful to hear you say once more, 'It's a good fire.'"

"Thank you," she says as I give her the coffee.

"Now the dream medicine." I pour in the brandy.

"I have to ask you one question, where is the axe?"

"The axe is outdoors. Out there in the rain. Axe in the rain. You know how it is with axes, how they wait around for dream employment."

"I'd feel a whole lot better if you'd go outside and hide the axe. Hide it somewhere I'd never think of looking. Would you do that for me?"

"Sure. But tell me, where wouldn't you think of looking?"

"Hide it somewhere good," she says.

"I know just the right place. Just yesterday I discovered this hiding place and I thought to myself, 'What a great hiding place. If I ever need to hide something, something like an axe for example, this certainly would be the right place.' Now I'm about to do just that, hide something, namely an axe. You can depend on me," I say.

"Go do it," she says.

I go outside. It's raining, coming down hard, and the wind's picked up. I take hold of the axe and stand under the overhang that provides shelter for the wood. I stand there holding the axe and watching the rain. Then I place the axe behind the woodpile.

"You weren't gone very long," Cheryl says when I go back in.

"It's hell out there," I reply.

"You just went outside and came in again. I asked you to hide the axe. To hide it, hide, as in to put something somewhere where someone can't find it. And you just went outside and came in again. I'm not an idiot. I'm a little freaked out by the nightmare but I'm not an idiot and I resent that you don't respect my request."

"The axe is where you'll never find it."

"The axe is right out there. All I have to do is go outside and it's there. I know it. It's just right outside the door. You're no help, no help at all. You're absolutely useless sometimes."

"I can chop wood and I can build a fire."

"But can you hide an axe? That's all I ask right now. Can you do that?"

"I've already done that. The axe is where you'll never find it. Rest assured."

"Don't let me go out there," she says in a shivering voice, her hand with the coffee cup beginning to tremble, shaking so badly that she spills the coffee on her nightie.

"I won't let you go out there," I say.

"If I go out there I'll find the axe and I'm scared I'll freak out."

"If you go out there you won't find the axe because I've hidden the axe in a secret hiding place, and besides I won't let you go out there. I won't let you go out there no matter what happens. You can count on me."

"I certainly hope so," she says with a shudder.

FIREMEN

In front of the fire station, the firemen, four big beefy guys with crew cuts, are sitting out in the afternoon sunshine while in our small ground floor apartment, directly across the street from the station, I've got Jimmy Hendrix on the stereo and I'm getting stoned, sitting in the shadows a bit back from the open window but near enough to look out because Jane, wearing a tie-dyed T-shirt and tight faded blue jeans with embroidered flowers, an outfit that accentuates her lean and hungry look, will be coming home soon.

I'm in the habit of witnessing the routine of the firemen's teasing, their derisive laughter, whistling, muted catcalls and comments about hungry looking hippies, free love, flower power, bra burning, all done in such a way you'd think they were simply goofing around among themselves, but of course loud enough to reach Jane's ears while she walks on our side of the street, just like their remarks making fun of our music and guys with beards and long hair are often loud enough to travel through the open window.

Jane puts on a good show of defiance, her head held high, long black hair streaming proudly, a graceful arrogance while she strides along, but when she enters our apartment she slams the door behind her, goes directly to the stereo and shuts off the music, shouting she just can't stand it anymore, can't stand my apathy, can't stand me sitting around all day with the music blasting, getting stoned.

As angry as she is she still lights incense and candles, her familiar ritual upon arrival. I offer her a hit from the joint, a tactic that sometimes works but not today, because today she's louder and angrier than usual and she just can't stand any of it, not the music, not the stale smell of marijuana, not the rednecks across the street with their insulting remarks, and especially not me sitting here all day indifferent to everything in the real world.

Glancing out the window, I can see the firemen's grinning faces fixed in the direction of our window. I start to close the window which only infuriates Jane the more, shouting, "Why are you closing the window?" To which I answer, "Because they can hear every word." And, her volume increasing, "Let them! Let them hear! Let the whole world hear." She pushes past me, shoves the window open, leaning out, shouting out to the firemen, "Go away, go away, please just go away."

And while I sit smoking with the music cranked up, she does just that, goes away. From the window I see her waiting for the taxi, standing proudly in her hiking boots, her backpack like a faithful dog at her feet, her rain jacket zipped up though the sun is shining. The firemen are now busily attending to their fire truck, the head honcho supervising them, so they are on good behavior, appearing oblivious to what is occurring with Jane.

The taxi pulls up and the driver turns out to be a replica of myself, a guy with long hair and a beard, treating her with every courtesy, placing her backpack in the trunk, opening the door to usher her into the back seat, and she pauses before settling in to begin her journey, looks one last time at our window but I'm in the shadows a bit back from the window so there's no one to wave to one last time, just a final toss of her head, tossing her hair back.

The firemen stare after the taxi until their chief commands them to get on with the task at hand, making the fire truck bright and shiny. The next days I stay in, the window closed, only soft music for company in my smoke-filled den, and glancing through the murky windowpanes I notice that the firemen are quieter than usual, almost penitent, staring sadly at my closed window.

BIKERS

We're living in a small house outside of town and on this stretch of road not much else other than the house we rent and a bar nearby that has become a bikers' hang-out. All night long the violence, the brawling revelry, the terrible machines shattering the hoped for peace, the bikers coming and going or just roaring up and down the road for the sheer hell of it.

"I can't stand another night of this," Mary cries out desperately, pulling at her hair, and as usual I go to comfort her with reassuring words about finding another place to live, but without warning she's gone, swift of foot out the door. Her white nightgown fluttering angelically behind her in the breeze, she wings down the road with me in hot pursuit, calling out breathlessly, "Come back, come back home where it's safe."

And by the time I do manage to catch up with her she has just barely escaped being run down by a demon in black leather, charging off to another orgiastic brawl down the road apiece. Like a runner on an obstacle course, Mary's manoeuvring through the throng of sinister, gleaming bikes parked randomly outside the road-house.

The brawny leather-clad bikers hanging around outdoors are engaged in the usual biker entertainment of fisticuffs, knife throwing, chain swinging, wrestling, dope smoking, along with some skimpily leather-clad biker damsels obviously not in distress who are cheering them on. They all take turns throwing their heads back and yelling curses at the top of their voices to the starry heavens, and obvious fornicating is taking place in the bushes.

Mary flashes ghostly by and they each give her a bleary-eyed disbelieving stare and I'm now right behind her while she stands before the bearded giant of a biker at the door. "Stop it, can't you just for one night stop it?" Her voice shrieks uncannily through the night, rising above the frenzy of screams, shouts, laughter, curses, all the mayhem interspersed with battering sounds of shattered glass and smashed furniture, the violence coming from within. Just at this moment some biker maidens, their leather garments partly torn open, burst nymph-like through the door, pursued by burly bearded bikers. They all stop, gawking in disbelief at Mary, barefooted, clad in her simple white nightgown, arms upraised, tears streaming down her face, shrieking, "Brutes, brutes all of you brutes and brutesses."

One biker with a strikingly blue-eyed, angelic countenance takes the time to pause. Stroking his beard thoughtfully, he casts his eyes kindly upon Mary and remarks, "Dear lady, don't you think that perchance you've stumbled into the wrong movie?"

As Mary, under the influence of the biker's radiant eyes, comes to a halt, I rush toward her in a somewhat forceful manner, intending to take her in my arms, to remove her from danger. "She doesn't mean it, she doesn't mean it. A case of temporary insanity, be merciful."

Before I know what's happening, a giant has lifted me off my feet, asking, "Do you batter your wife?"

Thank God Mary comes to her good senses, saying, "Unhand him, unhand my husband, for he's absolutely no wife beater, but you, you all, you're driving me crazy." Her shrieking is such that the bikers and biker women all move back, clearing a vibrant space around her, and, with a bit of a jolt, I'm once again set back on my feet.

The noise from inside grows even louder, brutal shouts, jubilant laughter, screaming pleasure, and Mary dashes through the door. I'm looking all around from one biker to another, asking permission, and biker blue eyes places his hand gently on my shoulder, saying, "Follow her, my brother." The giant steps away from the door and with a graceful bow ushers me in.

What's transpiring around us is the kind of bacchanalian, sinful goings-on that would have put Sodom and Gomorrah to shame. One of the damsels from outside, who has followed us in, claps Mary on the back in encouragement, saying "Do your thing, sister. Go talk to Mike the Viking over there."

Mary rushes up to Mike the Viking who's reclining on the couch, leather clad females curled up near him, and in her now familiar shrieking voice Mary pleads her case. "Lady," Mike the Viking says, "I get your drift. It is a bit noisy in here. Bikers, be soundless. Turn off the sound," Mike the Viking booms out and silence descends, complete and absolute silence, silence reigns. The orgy and the violence continue but soundless like a television in which the sound has been turned off.

"Happy now?" Mike the Viking asks and his voice is the last sound we hear in that place, other than the sounds we ourselves make, for the spell of the command obviously does not include Mary and I.

Then Mike the Viking grabs hold of a woman, gestures a command, and the woman begins a soundless bumping and grinding striptease dance, soundless laughter and soundless shrieks of pleasure rising from the onlookers, coming from them in waves of soundlessness, just as the orgiastic rites and violence continues as before only now without sounds of any kind.

"Let's go home dear," I whisper to Mary in my still audible voice and the whisper sounds preternaturally loud.

We huddle together trying to be as quiet as possible, making our way out the door, avoiding the soundless shattering of bottles and broken furniture, the soundless jubilant cries, and bodies hurtling soundlessly around us, soundless screams and soundless howls of pleasure.

The giant at the door grins at us and soundlessly enunciates the words, "You got what you came for. Go home and be kind to each other."

We wend our way back to our humble dwelling, manoeuvring through the bikes, staying clear of the soundless knife-throwing, the soundless fisticuffs and wrestling, the soundless chain swinging, and soundless fornicating, a biker soundlessly hopping into the saddle of his machine and soundlessly speeding by, almost soundlessly running us over.

Back in our peaceful home, how can we tear ourselves away from the windows, from the eerie spectacle of the soundless world of the bikers, just to lose ourselves in peaceful, ordinary sleep?

CLEM

I'm lying in bed when I hear a car screech to a stop on front of the house. I hear the sound of a man running on the cement walk and then the sound of the running man fades out and I hear high-heeled footsteps continuing along the cement walk. I hear a woman's voice. I hear my father speak a few words. I sit up in bed, the first time in many days that I have sat up, and I look out the window at the acres and acres of dark soil, the acres of dark soil under the gray sky, the soft drizzle of rain. But this time I don't see my father out there with his plow. I see a man in a suit, the man running, stumbling as the wet soil clutches at his shoes, the man falling, lying face down in the dark soil.

I get out of bed, put on my overalls, my boots, my old wool jacket that used to belong to my father and after all these years still smell of him. I go out my bedroom door, noticing that my father hasn't done much cleaning up since the day I decided to lie down and rest for my journey to the big city. I open the front door, step out onto the porch, and close the door behind me. I lean in the doorway, coughing a few times as I inhale the smoke from my father's pipe. He sits on the stairs just barely sheltered from the rain and the clouds of smoke rise from him. He puffs on his pipe and looks out over the dark soil in the direction of the man lying face down. And a blond-haired woman stands in the rain, stands on the cement walk, stands near the stairs like she's thinking of walking up them, of finding shelter, and she too stares out over the dark soil at the man lying face down out there.

She holds her gray wool coat close to her body, her arms folded, and I notice the necklace of pearls, the sparkling earrings, and when I cough she looks up at me. I look away from her. I look at the road, at the shiny black sedan, the two front doors sprawled wide open, and then I look at the woman again. She's still looking at me but I just stare right down at her red high heel shoes. She shifts around restlessly, the heels clicking on the cement walk.

"Some city slicker needed to get back to the soil. Happens to all of them once in a while, sooner rather than later I expect," my father says as he puffs on his pipe. He doesn't turn to look at me and I don't cough this time while I inhale the smoke.

I put my hands in the pockets of my old wool jacket and walk past my father, walk slowly down the few stairs, slowly striking my heels hard on the wooden stairs, and I stand close to the woman. I inhale her perfume. She wears red lipstick and a soft purple makeup around her eyes. I bring my weight down hard on the heels of my boots, shifting my weight from one heel to the other. We face each other. I look past her at the man lying face down in the soil.

Then I look straight into her eyes. "You didn't have to bring him here." I speak the words through clenched teeth, and she steps back, her heels clicking on the cement.

She glances nervously in the direction of the man. Her lips part but she's so nervous that she can't find the words right away. A cloud of pipe smoke floats between us. "It was the first place we saw, the first with such dark soil. All he wants is to get back ..."

"I said you didn't have to bring him here."

Then my father speaks. "What you and that woman talking about, Clem?"

And that's when I know. I know the time has come. I know there's no waiting any more. I turn away from the woman. I glance at the man lying face down out there in the dark soil. I inhale the smoke for the last time from my father's pipe.

Hunching over a bit as if to find some kind of shelter within myself from the rain, I walk down the cement path, walk out the gate, walk past the shiny black sedan with the doors wide open. I walk down the road and keep going.

AFTERNOON FOR ETERNITY

You are sitting in a small café when the woman appears. She speaks a language you have never heard but somehow you understand her. With enticing gestures she expresses her surprise at finding you sitting at this table, for it is her table where she sits every afternoon to write in her diary. Yet she is not displeased to find you here. You can tell this from her pleasurable laughter and tone of voice. She sits down, making clear that you must remain but not disturb her because she is here to write in her diary. You know right away that she will take you home with her. She sits close to you, leaning against you as she writes in her own language, and her excitement is a shared secret, her body pressing against yours, her muted laughter promising an intimate Shangri-La. Finally she closes her diary, looks at her watch, and you leave with her. She strides magnificently through the darkening streets, and you hurry along beside her. Everyone steps aside, the men bowing, taking off their hats in gallant gestures, women throwing flowers in her path. Though she pays you no attention, still she wants you there, and finally you come to a long flight of stone steps leading up to a villa. You follow her up the stairway that gets longer, steeper as you climb, but she goes ahead of you at an intoxicating pace, each step bringing you closer to the fulfillment of maddening delight. Darkness falls. You can barely make out the woman up ahead, but she waits for you at the top of the stairs. She smiles as she opens a door and enters. But as the door closes and the woman disappears, the villa disappears with her and you are all alone at the top of the long winding flight of stairs, just you and absolute darkness. A storm strikes, scathing rain, lightning, thunder, a fierce wind threatening to blow you away unless you lie down, which you do, clinging somehow to the threshold that leads to a plunge into the glowing darkness. But don't worry. You will see her again. These afternoons repeat and repeat.

ADMONITIONS

A happy couple who knows me quite well invites me over for a small dinner party. They want me to become acquainted with a woman, a good friend of theirs. They're certain that she and I will take to each other. The nice couple, they cook exquisite Chinese cuisine. As the evening progresses, what the woman and I have most in common is an inability to eat with chopsticks.

*

She says that she likes the afternoons. For her the afternoon is a silken surface. In the afternoon she always feels as if she is alive in a silk painting and she always wears a white silk blouse in the afternoon, lilac perfume, her jade necklace.

I ask her what she will be doing later.

"Don't ask me about later. You wouldn't want to know about later. Later is when I disappear from the face of the earth.""

*

The expected house guest telephones to remind me to leave the key underneath the doormat as we had agreed because I can't be at home to greet him when he arrives. But I'm having second thoughts about this arrangement and I say so. Silence ensues on his end. I explain that my neighbor's house had been broken into a few days before. I admit that I'm perhaps being unreasonably nervous about hiding my door key somewhere outside my house during my absence but really in light of recent developments it doesn't seem that my hesitation should be so difficult to comprehend. Such goings-on should indeed give one pause. And when he still utters no reply, I say, "Please don't think that you're to blame."

*

She accuses me of never willingly divulging information about myself. She says that I appear to be a man burdened by secrets.

I assure her that her perception of me is indeed accurate.

She urges me to have faith in our friendship, to trust her, to unburden myself by revealing to her what is so deeply troubling.

I look her straight in the eyes and decide to take a chance.

I confess that I have never learned to swim and therefore never take a summer holiday.

*

I go with two friends for a Sunday afternoon drive in the country. I sit alone in the back seat and it soon becomes clear to me that the manner in which the two friends converse between themselves exclude me completely.

I fall into a withdrawn, moody silence. They seem to have forgotten all about me.

We're already a good distance outside the city and I lose my bearings. The friend in the front passenger seat is in charge of the map and he gives directions where to turn, informs his friend the driver where we are, suggests which route to take, and so on.

Suddenly I blurt out, "Could you please give me the map?"

Silence ensues in the front seats.

"I'd like to take a look at the map," I say forcefully.

*

The chambermaid waiting in the corridor for the do-not-disturb signs to vanish in the storm of departing guests and I've had enough of getting out the door. Sitting next to my packed suitcase, looking around again and again to make sure nothing has been forgotten. This day going on wherever the day goes to become tomorrow is the only taxi I need to get wherever I'm journeying to. My own voice soon will blend with all the other voices in our coming and going, language in all directions, and all I need is to be kept like a diary.

*

As she's driving away in her car, a red sports car with the top down on this bright sunny afternoon, I call out, "Have fun."

I stand in the street, waving goodbye, waiting for the car to turn the corner and disappear from sight. But suddenly the car stops and backs up swiftly to where I am standing.

She lifts her sunglasses as she faces me. "Have fun," she snarls. "Just what do you mean by have fun?"

I assure her that I'd spoken with genuine goodwill.

She guns the engine and speeds off.

*

He's a strong, convincing conversationalist, and we all tend to agree with his opinions. Just the other day, for example, he informed us, in no uncertain terms, that he never makes plans. We answered that we completely understand, for in his place we would undoubtedly follow the very same course.

*

"What an ordeal," I said. Afterwards I realize that perhaps I hadn't responded appropriately.

A friend had been telling me about the night before. He'd been out dancing with a beautiful woman, danced the night away. Then to her place, champagne and wild sex until seven o'clock in the morning.

The beautiful woman had gotten out of bed, gone out for fresh rolls, exquisite cheese, fruit, returned and prepared a lavish breakfast.

By then my friend had been sleeping soundly in the queen-sized bed that he now had all to himself but of course the beautiful woman had insisted that he get out of bed and partake in sharing the special breakfast all nicely laid out, awaiting them on the balcony, indeed a wonderful sunny morning.

I have known my friend long enough to know that he detests the display of sitting out on sunny mornings, complacently having an elegant breakfast. And, anyway, he never eats breakfast.

Therefore, upon hearing his story: "What an ordeal." That's what I said.

*

A package arrives in the mail from a good friend who went off some months ago to visit the pyramids. The package is very light in weight and shaped unmistakably like a shoe box. I unwrap the brown paper wrapping and sure enough it is a shoe box. The shoe box is taped shut. The shoe box certainly feels empty. A note is scribbled on the cover of the box, the writing almost illegible. I manage to decipher the message, "Open at night alone in the dark for it was the same with me when I closed it."

*

I turn my head slightly to glance in the mirror and there isn't a mirror in that particular place on the wall where there certainly used to be a mirror and my surprise at there not being a mirror, my footsteps trip on the worn-out carpet.

*

Was a place. Some kind of place. The news kept coming in. We couldn't stop it. We might have wanted to. The news kept coming in. Like from everywhere. We made sense of it. Then it didn't matter. Everything was happening at the same time.

*

At the jazz club I sit at a secluded table. People arrive. They sit close to the stage. The musicians start playing. People keep coming in. Someone asks if it's

Ok to take a chair from my table. "It's not in use. Go ahead, take the chair." This particular someone goes off with the chair to find a more favorable location. Then someone else, "Is this chair free?" "Yes, it's unoccupied. You may take the chair." And off goes the chair to be placed closer to the music. Then another customer. "Can I take this chair?" "Yes, you can take the chair. No one's using it." I had thought there were just a few empty chairs at my secluded table but I must have been mistaken because the asking and taking of chairs goes on all night at the jazz club.

*

The golden face of the clock on the church tower catches the morning sun, and as I am hurrying by, late for an appointment, I glance up to read the time, except there isn't any time, only a stunning golden reflection of the sun's rays. The clock's hands and numbers lost to my human perception, time invisible, a golden dazzling explosion of light. I stop in the middle of the sidewalk, my eyes raised as if to the heavens. The tower itself, there in the spotlight, seems to reach higher and higher. Though jostled now and then by people in a hurry, I am incapable of going on. And my surroundings slip into a hazy dream.

*

You used to exist in a special place in my thoughts where I'd carry on a constant conversation with you knowing that when I next saw you, a regular occurrence in those days, I'd just repeat the words all over again to you in person. But now, although the place is still there and you're long gone, I still like going to this special place in my thoughts where you used to be, except now I'm learning how to silently communicate with The No One There.

*

I call this place where I now live, I call it home, but I don't expect I will die here. I open the door. Come in. Everything exactly as I'd left it. Arriving home shortly before dawn, turning on some music, sitting in my easy chair, I find myself, instead of reflecting on the wonderful party I'd just come from, or on feeling the freshness of the approaching dawn, I find myself thinking about the innumerable times I have come in through the door. Putting the key in the lock, opening the door, coming in, setting on some music, pouring a glass of wine, or some other activity, depending on my needs at the time of day. But the door, the opening of the door, my return to the eternal silence taking place on a daily basis, the experience of everything exactly as I'd left it. There will never be a first time anymore.